D1274503

Romeo

and the

Beastly
Bullies

ISBN 978-1-0980-1954-9 (paperback)
ISBN 978-1-0980-1956-3 (hardcover)
ISBN 978-1-0980-1955-6 (digital)

Copyright © 2019 by Silvia Beck Speyer

All rights reserved. No part of this publication may be reproduced, distributed, or transmitted in any form or by any means, including photocopying, recording, or other electronic or mechanical methods without the prior written permission of the publisher. For permission requests, solicit the publisher via the address below.

Christian Faith Publishing, Inc.
832 Park Avenue
Meadville, PA 16335
www.christianfaithpublishing.com

Printed in the United States of America

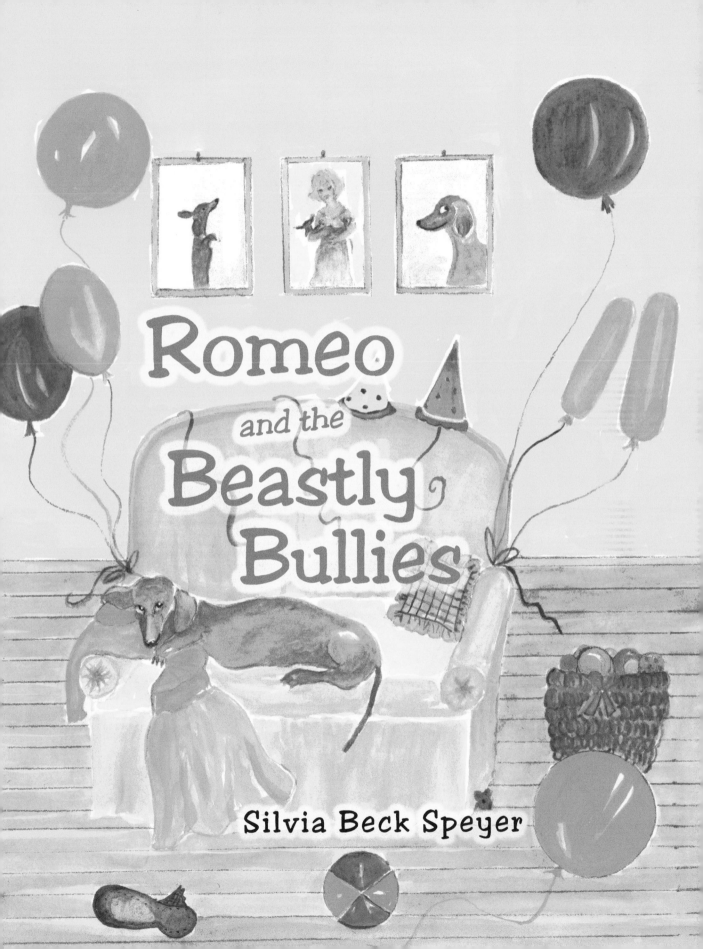

Romeo
and the
Beastly
Bullies

Silvia Beck Speyer

Every day, Romeo, a friendly dachshund, strolled through his neighborhood, looking for friends. When Big Boy, a Saint Bernard dog, and his buddies spotted Romeo, they growled at him and called him names.

One morning, Big Boy yelled, "Hey, wiener dog! Next time, I'll jump over my fence and bite you!"

Romeo dashed around the corner where he bumped into Chap and Miss Strudel.

"Hey, did somebody shrink your legs?" teased Miss Strudel, the poodle.

Chap, the Lab, snarled, "You would make a great speed bump!"

"You're not better than me just because you are bigger! My teeth are sharp and I can balance a ball on my nose!" Romeo cried. Miss Strudel shook her fluffy hairdo and snapped at Romeo.

Why is everybody so nasty? Romeo wondered. He raced home and snuggled in his cozy blanket. He thought, *If I get treats for them, they will like me.*

The next morning, Romeo ran into the bullies again and said, "I can get us many biscuits with my balancing act!"

"Get lost! We're after that burglar who has been breaking into our homes!" Chap pushed Romeo into the dirt.

"You're nothing but a pack of bullies!" Romeo yelled. Then he limped home.

Romeo hopped on Miss Julia's lap where he always found comfort, the perfect place to daydream.

If I could fly…

If I could be scary like a wolf...

If I could ride in a police car...

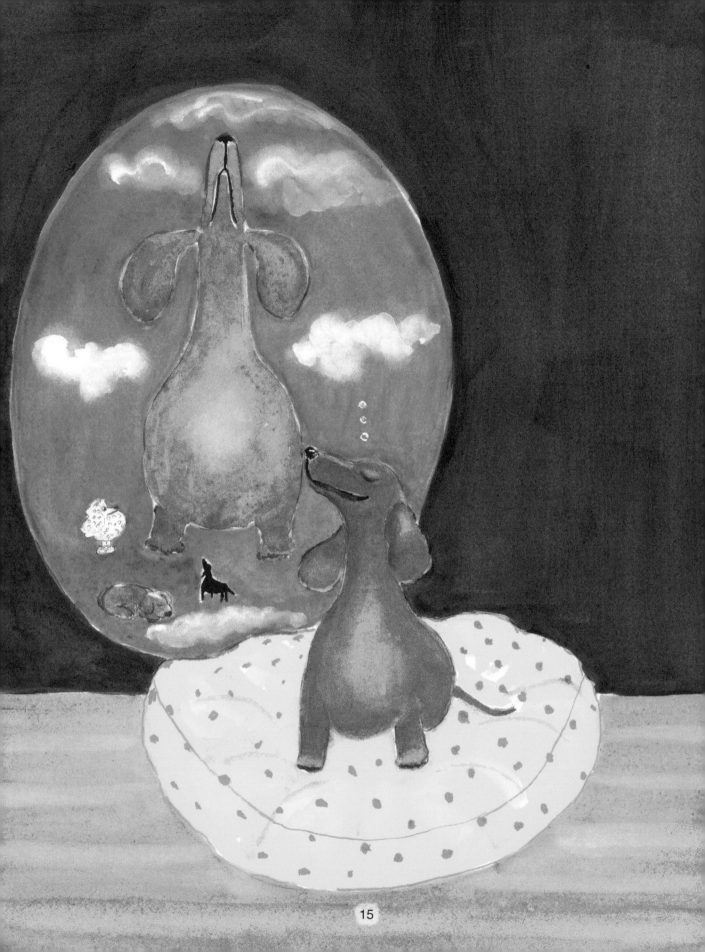

If I was the biggest dog in the world,
I could catch that burglar!

The next day, the burglar broke into Romeo's house! Romeo lunged at the burglar and bit into his boot.

The burglar cried, "Ouch!" He dropped the bag with the money he had stolen from Big Boy's house and crashed through the window.

Big Boy, Chap, and Miss Strudel had followed the burglar to Romeo's house and were waiting for him outside. Chap pushed the burglar down, Big Boy put his paws on his chest, and Miss Strudel howled as loud as a wolf. Meanwhile, Miss Julia called the police. Officer Jim came quickly and arrested the burglar.

The burglar's boot became Romeo's favorite chew toy because it reminded him of his great deed when he and his new friends caught the bad burglar.

Everybody in the neighborhood was happy that the burglar had been caught. They gave Romeo a party with more toys and treats he had ever seen. Even the bullies were invited.

Miss Strudel said, "Thanks for inviting us, but we can't stay. It's dinnertime. We just want to tell you that we're very proud of you. You're a big dog in a little body!"

"Romeo!" Miss Julia called. "You were so brave! You deserve a steak!" She gave Romeo a pat on the head and a yummy steak.

Romeo had an idea.

He rushed down the lane to where the three dogs had gone. "Thanks for helping catch the burglar," Romeo said. Now that we are friends, I want to share my steak with you."

"Wow! Thank you!" The bullies licked their chops.

Then Chap asked, "Romeo, will you show us your trick with my ball?"

Romeo was a sensation with his balancing act.

Romeo asked, "Why were you so mean to me?"

"We are really sorry. We were bored," Big Boy said. Chap and Miss Strudel nodded.

30

"Officer Jim wants to reward us and take us on a ride in his cruiser," Romeo said.

They all agreed that it would be great fun to ride around in a police car.

From that day on, the four dog heroes patrolled the streets with Officer Jim, and no burglars dared to come to their neighborhood ever again.

About the Author

Silvia Beck Speyer lives in Pittsburgh, Pennsylvania, where she raised her two children. She divides her time between tending to her award-winning garden, painting, and writing children's books. Her five-year-old miniature dachshund, Romeo, inspired her to write this story. He is brave, affectionate, and truly a "big dog in a little body."